31172036692168

The Mystery of EATUM HALL

Horace & Glenda Pork-Fowler
DUNFASTIN
GLUTTONS WAY

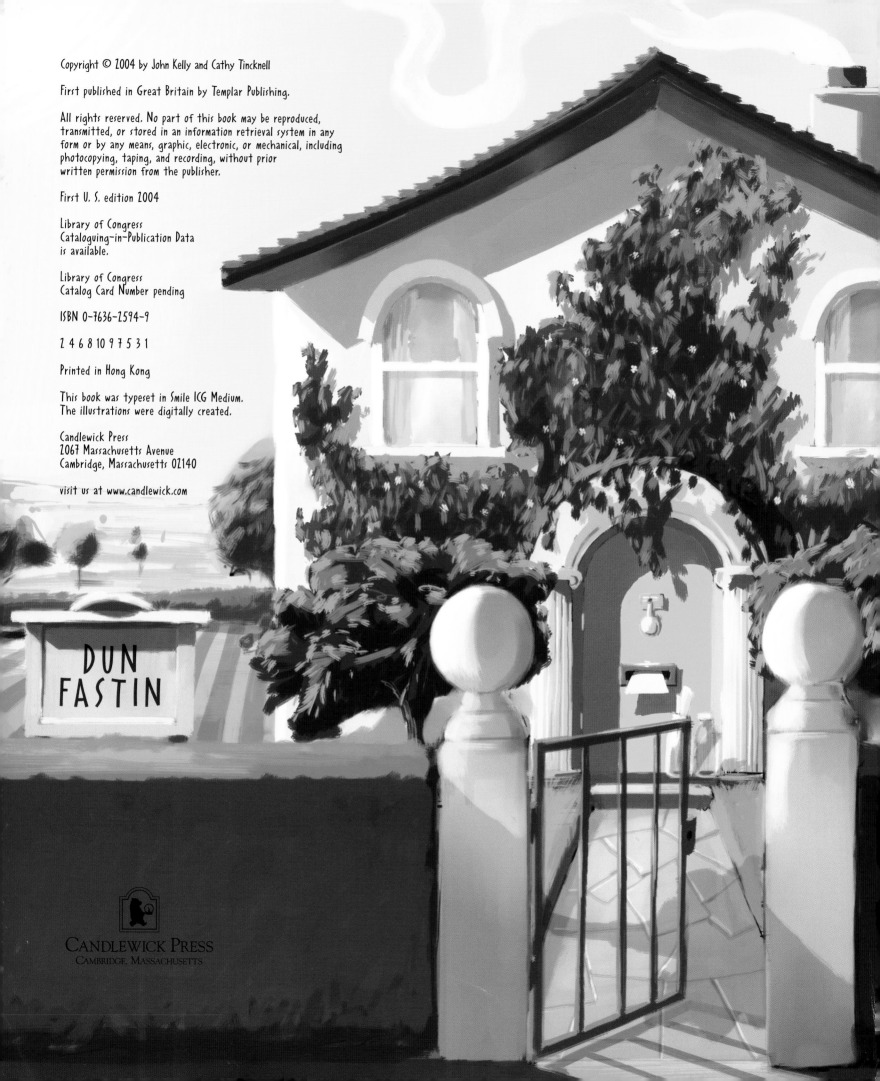

First U. S. edition 2004

Library of Congress
Cataloguing-in-Publication Data
is available.

Library of Congress
Catalog Card Number pending

ISBN 0-7636-2594-9

2 4 6 8 10 9 7 5 3 1

Printed in Hong Kong

This book was typeset in Smile ICG Medium.
The illustrations were digitally created.

Candlewick Press
2067 Massachusetts Avenue
Cambridge, Massachusetts 02140

visit us at www.candlewick.com

CANDLEWICK PRESS
CAMBRIDGE, MASSACHUSETTS

DUN
FASTIN

The Mystery of EATUM HALL

John Kelly and Cathy Tincknell

GLUTTONS WAY

After an excellent breakfast, a jolly nice letter arrived from Dr. Hunter, the new owner of Eatum Hall.
He was inviting Glenda and me for a weekend of free gourmet food!

It was to begin that very night, so Glenda had only seven hours to pack. We'd have just enough time for an afternoon snack before we set off!

We had a bracing drive up to Eatum Hall, though Glenda was
slightly spooked by the old road through the woods.
She was convinced there were strange noises
out there. Silly bird!

It was my tummy rumbling!

I must say it was a bit of a disappointing welcome,
with the door wide open, and no lights, staff,
or food anywhere to be seen.

We were about to turn tail for home
when Glenda spotted a note
on the hallway table.

It was addressed to
Horace and Glenda Pork-Fowler.

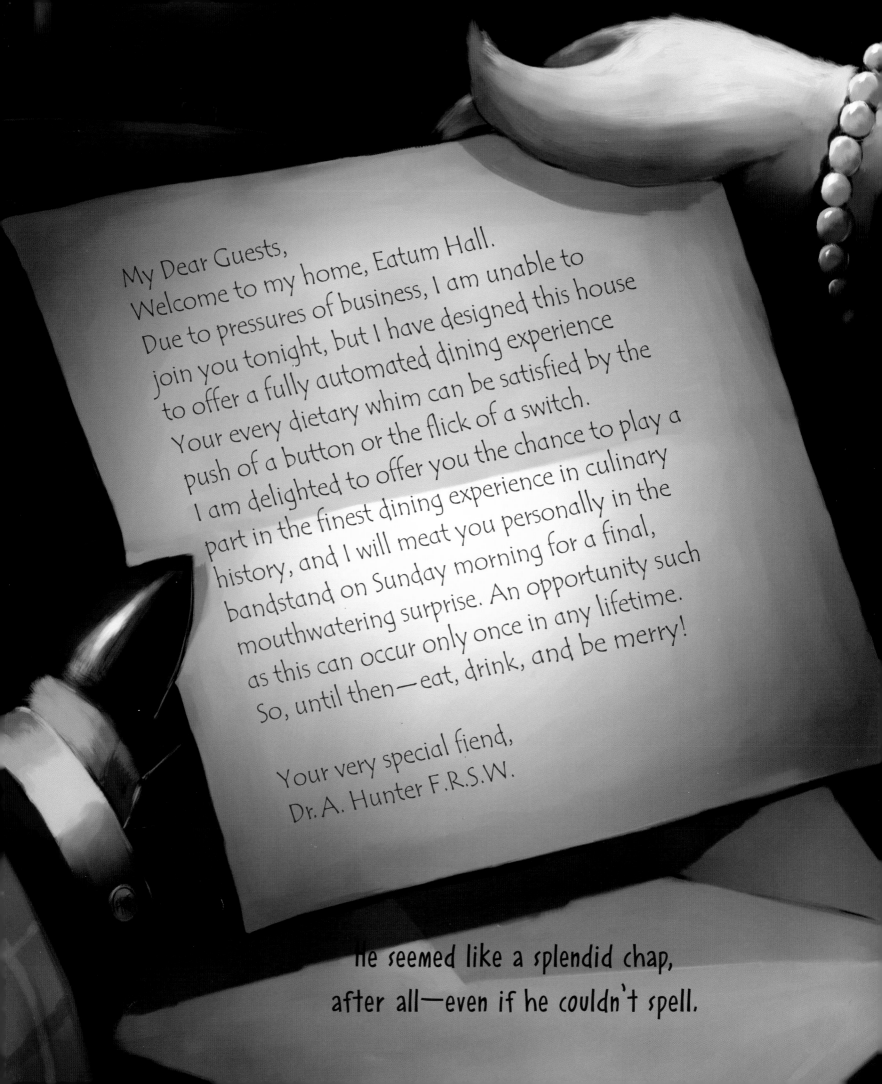

My Dear Guests,

Welcome to my home, Eatum Hall.

Due to pressures of business, I am unable to join you tonight, but I have designed this house to offer a fully automated dining experience. Your every dietary whim can be satisfied by the push of a button or the flick of a switch.

I am delighted to offer you the chance to play a part in the finest dining experience in culinary history, and I will meat you personally in the bandstand on Sunday morning for a final, mouthwatering surprise. An opportunity such as this can occur only once in any lifetime. So, until then—eat, drink, and be merry!

Your very special fiend,
Dr. A. Hunter F.R.S.W.

He seemed like a splendid chap,
after all—even if he couldn't spell.

We went to our rooms to change for dinner.
Dr. Hunter seemed to be a bit of a collector as
well as a scientist. Glenda was fascinated by the
works of art displayed on the walls, but I told her,
"I prefer MY works of art displayed on a plate."

Ha, ha, ha!

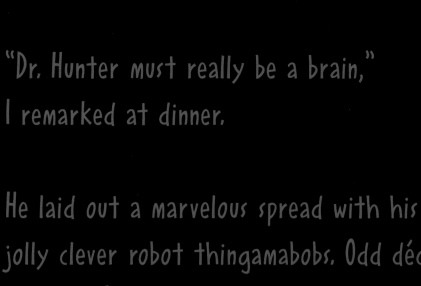

"Dr. Hunter must really be a brain,"
I remarked at dinner.

He laid out a marvelous spread with his
jolly clever robot thingamabobs. Odd décor,
though. Glenda was not at all impressed, but
I thought the portrait over the fireplace was
rather good—especially the way the eyes
seemed to follow our every move.

Proper art, I say!

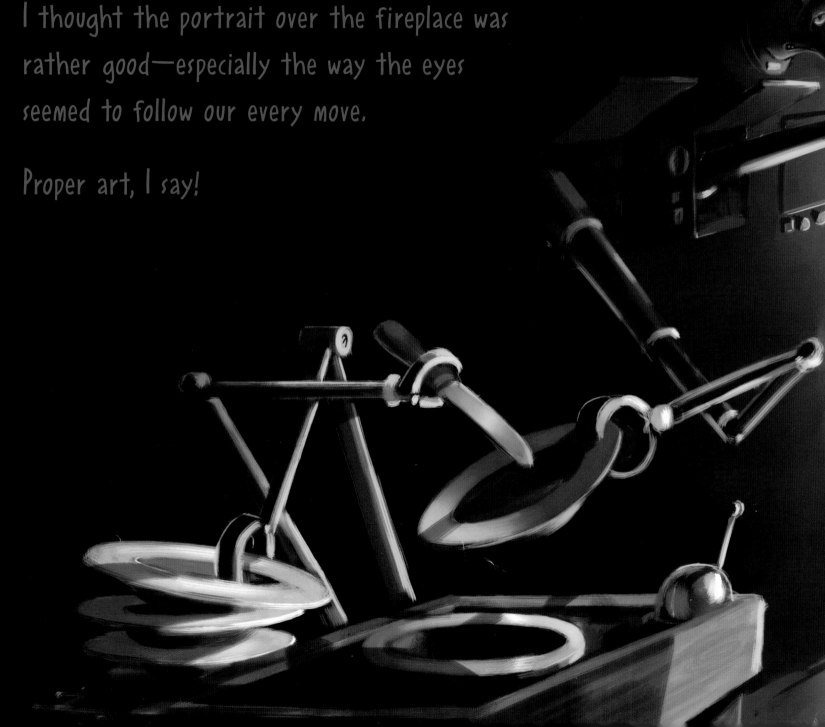

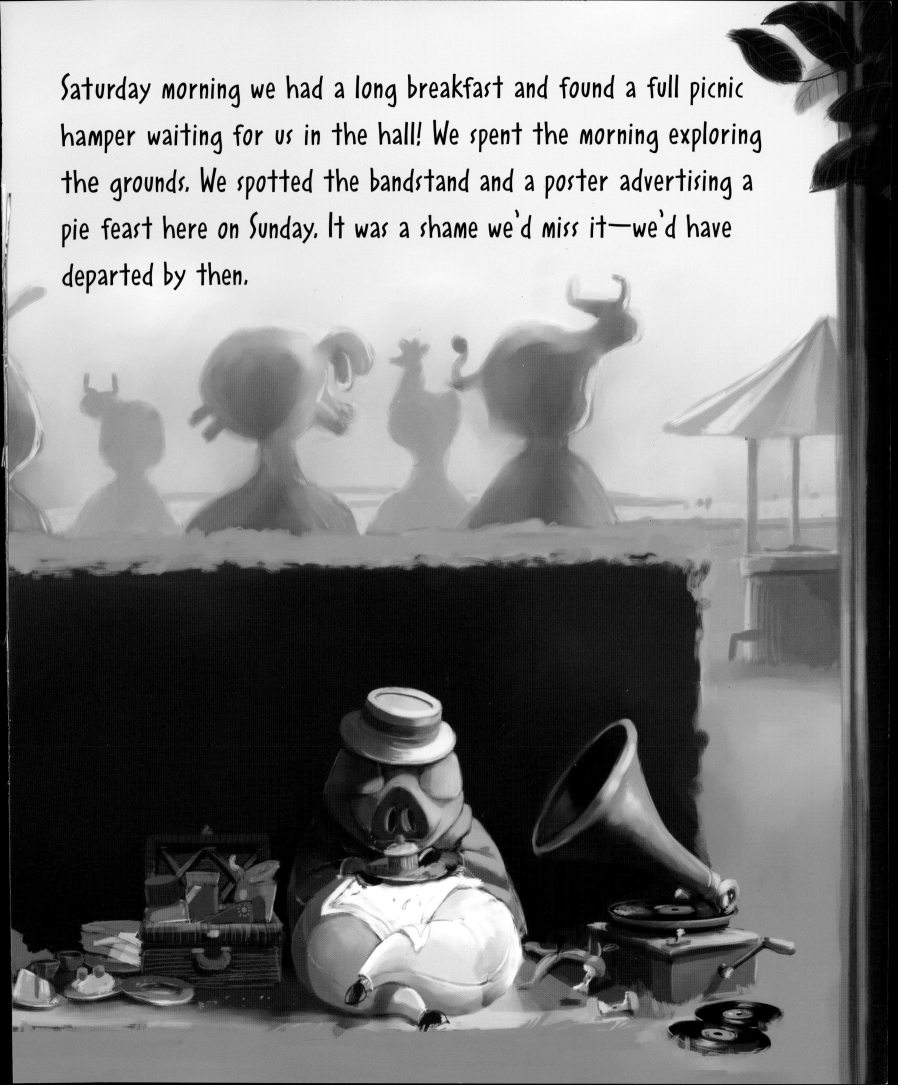

Saturday morning we had a long breakfast and found a full picnic hamper waiting for us in the hall! We spent the morning exploring the grounds. We spotted the bandstand and a poster advertising a pie feast here on Sunday. It was a shame we'd miss it—we'd have departed by then.

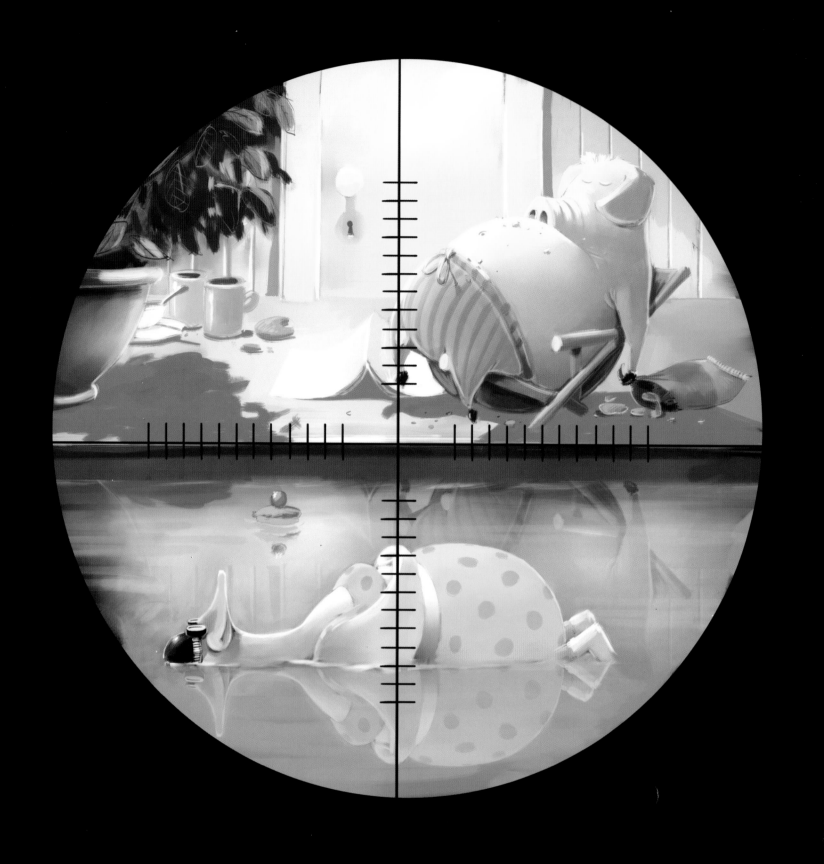

The rest of the day passed in a blur of wonderful nonstop food.
We did a bit of exercise and managed to work up a
respectable appetite for our evening meal.

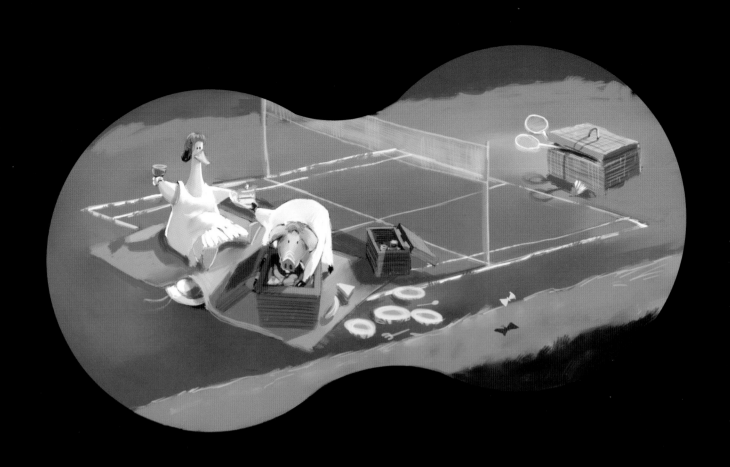

We were so full, I didn't even eat dessert. First time ever!

That night I thought to close my eyes for a few seconds while Glenda applied her lotions. But when I opened them again, the old girl was snoring contentedly beside me. My stomach, however, was far from content. It was grumbling. I decided I'd pop downstairs for a tiny snackette.

It was a long hike to the kitchen. You'd think a clever chap like Dr. Hunter would've put in an elevator. And there were far too many locked doors throughout the place! I was ravenous by the time I found the kitchen.

2 Pie-lid drops to secure meal in tin
1 Tempt food inside
3 Tin drops down
4 Furnace Ignites
(Cooking time: Approx 6 hours)
DANGER!
FILLING SHOULD NOT EXCEED RECOMMENDED WEIGHT

It was odd there was no light in the kitchen and no robot helpers, either. I had to fend for myself. Dr. Hunter was obviously a keen cook, though. The capital chap kept a very well-stocked fridge.

I went back to bed eventually—with
a few midnight treats for Glenda!

The next day, Sunday, after a leisurely final breakfast, we made our way to the bandstand. I have to say it was very poorly constructed and swayed most alarmingly as we climbed.

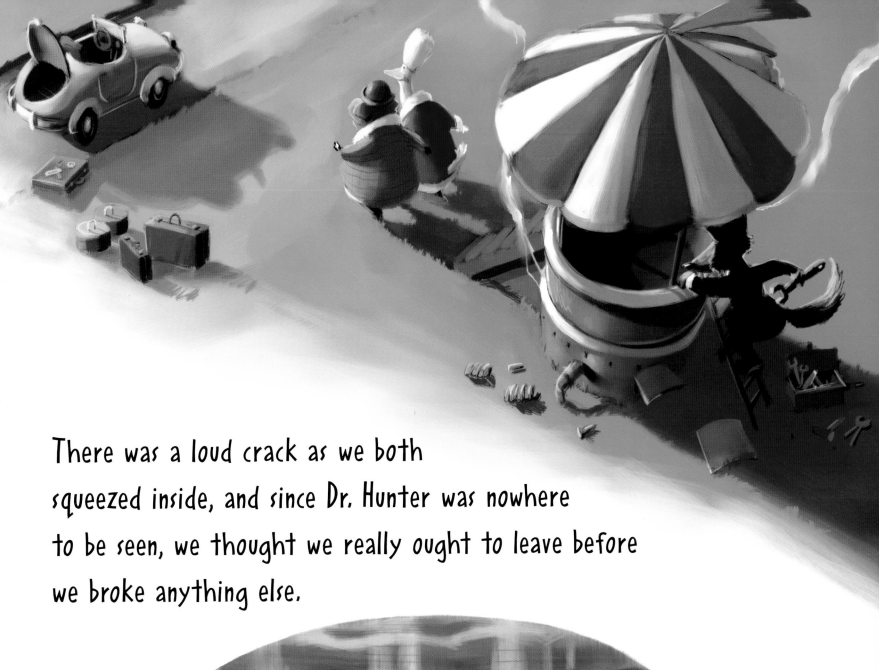

There was a loud crack as we both
squeezed inside, and since Dr. Hunter was nowhere
to be seen, we thought we really ought to leave before
we broke anything else.

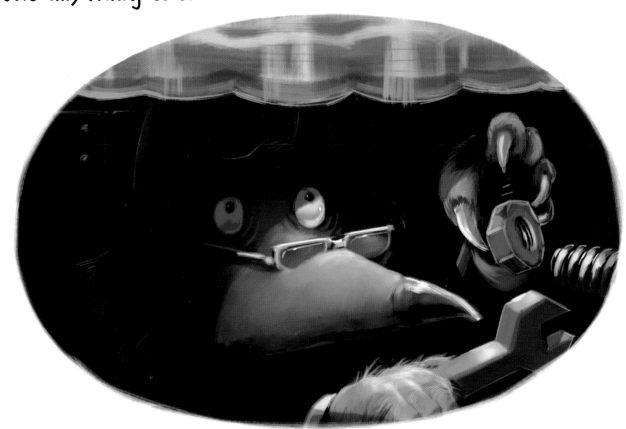

Although we searched for Dr. Hunter, we couldn't find him and decided to set off. We hoped to get home in time for a late lunch.

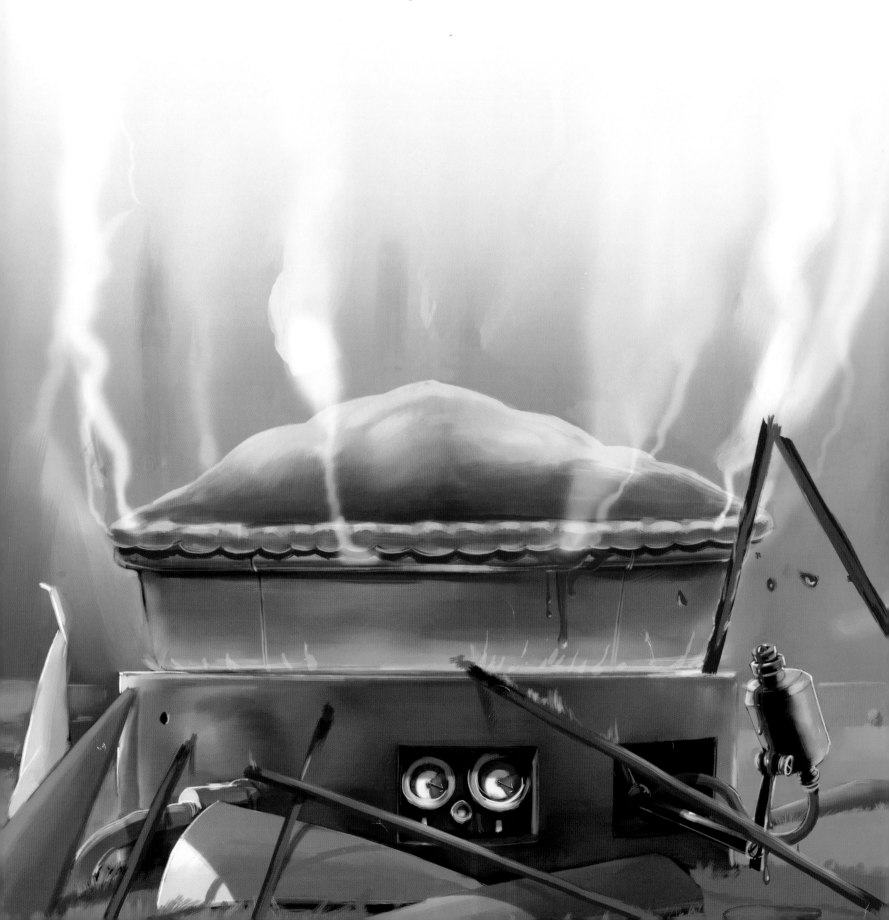

As we left, a coach full of guests was arriving for the pie feast. Dr. Hunter must have been too busy making arrangements to give us our surprise.

Never mind.

But it's a shame we never got to say goodbye, and thank you, of course! I wonder just what sort of pie they had?

The END